'So I'm lying bollock naked on Lola's rug.'

Lola is an artist and photographer with a particular interest in the power of the phallus. She thinks art should be challenging; Jed isn't quite so sure. So Lola decides to dispense with the theory and takes Jed home for a spot of practice to a backing of The Essential Leonard Cohen...

First published by Leaf Books Ltd in 2006
Copyright © Shelagh Middlehurst

Cover illustration © David Fisher

Leaf Books are proud to be working with
The University of Glamorgan

www.leafbooks.co.uk

Leaf
GTi Suite,
Valleys Innovation Centre,
Navigation Park,
Abercynon,
CF45 4SN

Printed by Allprint
www.allprint.ltd.uk

ISBN 1-905599-17-X
ISBN 9-781905-599172

Sex with
Leonard Cohen

by

Shelagh Middlehurst

Shelagh Middlehurst lives in Cardiff with three greyhounds and a husband. She has a number of poems and short stories published in small press magazines, with two more poems due to be published soon. She also has a short story in the latest Honno Anthology entitled *My Cheating Heart*.

Sex with Leonard Cohen

Through the haze of my reconstructed youth I see her come in. From a distance she's eighteen, as she gets closer, twenty-five. By the time she stands next to me and orders a drink, I can see she's over thirty. Long dark hair, red lips. I clear my throat and she turns, not seeing me. She's got one of those off-centre faces, the kind that looks not just through you, but beyond you. The kind that's on another planet. However, she's wearing a short skirt and fuck-me shoes. A feral female. I get a warm glow in my crotch and my mouth takes it from there.

'Let me,' I say, paying for her drink.

She sees me and widens her eyes. They remind me of the marbles I used to play with as a boy, green glass flecked with amber. The look is cautious but not unfriendly.

'Jed,' I offer my hand, 'alone in a strange land.'

'Lola.' She squeezes my fingers. Long red

nails graze my palm.

She's full of surprises. Like she's an artist and photographer.

'And I thought you were a model.' The old clichéd come-on hangs, stale in the air, threatening to poison the beginnings of a beautiful friendship. Then she laughs, full-throated. And I like the sound.

'You,' she tells me, 'are full of crap.' I agree with her and order more drinks.

I'd returned to the old port where I was born reluctantly: too many changes. The once working waterfront is now a tourist attraction. Fashionable shops, cafes, even an art gallery. I preferred the rotten-toothed old crone myself, but that's a personal opinion. This place is still the same though, almost. Only the crowd is different. Younger, louder. Or maybe I'm just older. Last orders find me and Lola deep in conversation about performance art and some crazy French woman who undergoes plastic surgery on camera. Without anaesthetic. The whole experience and the resulting video is the work of art.

'Exhibitionism. Sado-masochistic clap-trap. She must get off on the whole weird experience.' My critical faculties are, as usual, short and to the point.

'Maybe through her pain and transformation, we are supposed to learn something. By a vicarious process. She articulates and expresses our need, our yearning to tear off the mask of our mundane selves and discover the person within. The person we are afraid of becoming. Even if she makes herself conventionally ugly in the process.'

'I don't buy it, Lola, I'm old-fashioned. Art is about beauty as well as self expression. Okay, maybe there is all this angst with some artists, but you wouldn't want their stuff hanging on your living room wall. I think they should sort out their psychological problems and stop trying to con the public that it's Art.'

'So you don't think Art should be challenging? Asking questions? Giving us a new perspective on the world? Do you really think it's all about pretty pictures and the status quo?'

'No, I'm not saying that, not exactly.' I'm on shaky ground, and I know it.

'I think Tracy Emin's bed deserved to win the Turner Prize,' Lola says, warming to her subject. 'I reckon if she'd painted it and entered the painting, rather than the actual bed, people would have been able to stomach it. Van Gogh painted his bed and it does have poignancy, a sort of lonely stillness. Tracy's bed though makes you feel like an intruder in her personal space, her hell. There is an element of voyeurism, but at the same time we identify with her humanity.' She laughs and drains her glass.

'Lecture over, come on Jed, walk me home.'

She leads me through narrow back alleys between old warehouses. I smell damp wood, wet brickwork and wonder why these buildings are still standing. She tells me they are the temporary home of a group of artists; studios and exhibition space. But not for much longer.

Her studio is clutter and informal comfort. Paintings propped up against the walls, books in haphazard piles on the floor, cushions and throws on old-fashioned furniture.

I sit on a saggy sofa drinking red wine while she shows me photographs.

'Men's penises! You take pictures of dicks?' I flip through the photos of young and old, flaccid, semi-erect and fully engorged dicks. I feel like women must feel when confronted by page three bare breasts. Do I measure up?

'The phallus has been depicted in art for centuries,' Lola explains, 'but usually in its potent state. I'm interested in all its states, from acorn to oak tree. Men set such store by the power of the phallus, but there is a taboo associated with it and generally it's kept well hidden. I am interested in other parts of the body too though, the tender little nooks and crannies, so easily overlooked. The back of the knee, the inside of the elbow, the hollow of the neck. And wrists. Men's wrists can be so erotic.'

I look at her closely. And she's not joking.

'Is that why I'm here?'

'Strip, and I'll tell you.'

So I'm lying bollock naked on Lola's rug. 'Do I pass?' I'm surprised just how much I want her to say yes. She examines me. Quiet, focused.

'Your torso is heavy and dark. I like that. But, you see here, the loins…' She strokes my stomach low down, tracing my hip bones and where my thighs join my body. 'This is delicate; the skin is pale under the hair. It makes me want to put my lips on it.'

'Please do,' I croak.

'First I must photograph that wonderful erection.' She fetches a digital camera and takes my picture; then takes off her clothes. Her flesh is soft, with the earthy sweet smell of ripe fruit.

'Indulge my fantasy,' she says, getting up and putting a CD into the player. *The Essential Leonard Cohen* growls to life.

'I thought he was dead.'

'No, but he is an icon. Like Bob Dylan. Besides, you don't have to like his music or his philosophy. Just fuck me to the sound of his voice. Or is that too difficult?'

It's not difficult, once I get over the intensity of her response to his disembodied droning. It's like she doesn't need me. Doesn't need anyone. It's just her – and him.

'His voice crawls up my thighs. Right into here.' She places my hand on her warm soft flesh.

I'm over excited and come quickly and fiercely. I keep moving till her throaty climax mingles with his lyrics. The music stops, and we sleep.

Morning is in the room when I wake. I dress to the sound of Lola's breathing. She is small. Vulnerable in sleep. At the door, I turn, scribble my mobile number on the pad next to her phone.

On second thoughts I take Leonard Cohen out of the CD player. Slip him into my pocket. And leave.

About Leaf Books

Our mission is to provide readers with a pocket-sized read in the places where they are waiting, relaxing, taking a break. We aim to support writers by giving them a new market for their short stories and short non-fiction.

Don't forget to visit our website www.leafbooks.co.uk to tell us what you think of this book and to learn more about the writer and our other services.

Enjoy!

For more information about Leaf Books and our services, please visit our website:

www.leafbooks.co.uk

- Complete List of Leaf Books
- Writers' Biographies
- Readers' Forum
- Ebooks
- Audio Books
- MP3 Downloadable Books
- Stockists
- How to Submit a Story to Leaf
- Competitions
- Writers' Services
- Jobs with Leaf

Competitions and Submissions

The Leaf competition and submission calendar enables us to gather stories, non-fiction, poetry written by new and established writers in the UK and abroad.

Every entry or submission is read by at least two members of our readers' panel. The panel consists of book and story lovers who represent a wide selection of backgrounds and tastes. We are very proud of this selection procedure and believe it gives a fair chance to every writer who sends us their work.

'I never thought I could want again. That it was possible to love and need like the first time...'

Des danced the quickstep with Margie at the Waldorf Astoria in New York. Will he ever pluck up the courage to ask Alice to be his partner?

First published by Leaf Books Ltd in 2006
Copyright © Ruth Joseph

Cover illustration © David Fisher

Leaf Books are proud to be working with
The University of Glamorgan

www.leafbooks.co.uk

Leaf
GTi Suite,
Valleys Innovation Centre,
Navigation Park,
Abercynon,
CF45 4SN

Printed by Allprint
www.allprint.ltd.uk

ISBN 1-905599-17-X
ISBN 9-781905-599172

Tea-dance at the Waldorf Astoria

by

Ruth Joseph

Ruth Joseph's first collection *Red Stilettos* includes prize winning entries from the Rhys Davies and Lichfield Short Story competitions. She has had work published by *New Welsh Review*, Parthian, Honno, Loki, *Cambrensis*, and *The Western Mail Magazine*.

Her memoir *Remembering Judith*, which chronicles her life as a child-carer to an anorexic mother, has been published by Accent Press and was featured in *the Guardian*. She lives in Cardiff and adores her husband Mervyn, family and rescue-labrador Bobbi.

Tea-Dance at the Waldorf Astoria

I never thought I could want again. That it was possible to love and need like the first time. She, the woman who rules my mind and also my body, Alice that is, is sitting on the next table to me. It's Wednesday, 23rd of September, the Tea-dance at the Waldorf. No, not the posh London hotel with its sparkling lights clustering the staircases and waiters skimming around the edge of that beautifully sprung dance floor – bet you it's maple. And certainly not the Waldorf Astoria Hotel in New York, where Margie and I spent five blissful days on our honeymoon. Oh, what memories! We sneaked a quick couple of steps and chasses of a foxtrot through the Silver Corridor – you should have seen the black and white checked marble floor. Shining? You could see your face in it. The black and white vaulted ceiling, Deco arches sculpted in the roof, their vast curves

lit by enormous glittering chandeliers. And palms, huge potted palms, reflected in long mirrored windows. That was the place, dipped in history where the Astors, the Vanderbilts and the Guggenheims talked, danced and embraced. And I danced with her, our bodies close, touching all the time. I was aching with the want of her and I was much younger then, of course. I looked into those beautiful eyes, took her hand in mine and said,

'Hey girl when we're dancing, you're my Ginger and I'm your Fred.'

Vicky says I can see the Waldorf on the internet if I want, round at her house. But I'm not sure I do. It's safer wrapped up in the softness of reminiscence. I may not cope with the pain. When was it? When did I go to New York? Must be – gosh – time flies, was in 1978. I was forty. All that time ago – nearly twenty seven years and I haven't been, haven't touched – well obviously I've looked. It wouldn't be natural if I didn't. A man's got to look hasn't he? But I've never felt the need to go with another woman. It would have to be special,

like it was with Margie, and no other woman has ever made me feel quite the same. That is, until now. Would you like to see Margie? I've got a picture. I always carry it in my wallet – more valuable than money, that. Taken on a day out in Porthcawl. Look at her black silken hair hanging down to her shoulders. She'd catch it up at the sides in combs. We didn't worry about the environment in those days: she had tortoiseshell then. When the sun caught her locks, they shone like polished glass. And her eyes, very unusual, pale green eyes, the colour of mountain water when it ran over a reed bed to tumble into the deep of a trout pool. But my daughter kept saying, well, nagging sometimes: Margie's gone. I've got to face it, and that's why she's pushed me out to go dancing.

'Go on, Dad,' she said, 'You're a long time dead and if you don't start soon…'

Then she went on about how I'd never meet anyone attractive up at the allotment. Old Betti's the only woman member, and although our veg are lovely she would rather see me

happier and buy the veg from the market like everyone else.

'A bit more time out, Dad. Stuff the weeds and the winter planting. You'll meet a nice type of woman there, at the tea-dance,' she said.

Anyway the Waldorf that I go to is certainly not as grand as that New York place – that's part of an old dream that's danced right into the past now. No, it's the Waldorf Hotel in Swansea, just off Wind Street, away from the noisy part. And here I am, on the next table to Alice.

We were introduced to each other at the very beginning and we all had to wear stickers with our names on so that we could learn them quickly. I saw her name straight away, 'Alice', and then I ignored everybody else's. But she always seemed to be with a crowd. I think she'd been before. They all seemed to know her and up until now I haven't had the courage to speak.

So up until now I haven't spoken to her, Alice, that is. We've nodded a couple of times. She's

got a lovely smile and when she dances, although she's not a small woman, she skims across the floor with such lightness. Like the puff of the seeds of a dandelion clock. And holds herself with such a straight back. I can remember my mother sending all the girls to ballet when they were young because the training would give them straight backs.

If I could smile at Alice again, maybe when the tea comes round at half-time, I could offer her one of my sandwiches. There again each of the tables is groaning with a wonderful spread. But I must pluck up the courage to talk to her somehow.

I look at that wonderful curve of her body. Such a slim waist – they used to call that an hour-glass figure – not skinny like the modern fashion. She's a woman in the prime of her life, like a perfect cauli with a full wonderful creamy curd, about to be harvested.

'Thank you, ladies and gentlemen.'

That's the MC calling – the end of the dance. Time to go over. Go on Des, Just do it. But my legs are leaden and I'm gazing at a princess

– no, a queen and she may laugh at me.

Was tea over that quickly?

Damn it. Dai's got her now. And he'll hog her like last week till the very last dance. He's shufflin' and pantin' and pushing her round like an old steam engine. She's smiling so she must be happy.

I try to forget that she's in Dai's arms. Damn it, I really thought I would get there in time. They are turning and kind of twirling in a huff and puff sort of way and she's got an expression like she's alright with it. She's talking to him. Now, she's looking over at me. I could break in now. I could take her in my arms. Put one hand about that trim waist. Feel the softness of that hand in mine. We would be as one. Dancing as one. The foxtrot, the tango – how I love the tango. There's a sexy little dance. So close, like making love with clothes on. Good Lord what am I thinking? He's panting past again. I'm sure she's looking at me. Did she glance my way?

I dream of dancing the tango with her. She'd be wearing a stretchy dress of black sequins

– very classy, cut out; revealing some of her glorious breasts and the dress would be split down the side to almost indecent. Oh we'd dance, so close, that our bodies would be almost skin to skin and then, and then, she's whisperin' in my ear

'Why don't you come back for a bit of tea?'

And I'd go back to her place – apple pie neat, tidy as a pin, and it would be slow and perfect. She'd draw the curtains but we would still hear the muffled peace of birdsong. She'd pull me on the sofa with her eyes dewy pools and my hands would be gentle and touching her arms, sliding down to the soft warmth of her breasts and …Oh my Lord…

'Thank you, Ladies and Gentlemen. I do hope you've enjoyed today's tea-dance at the Waldorf Swansea. We shall be repeating this very successful event next week at the same time and, due to the popularity of this event we would recommend that you buy your tickets now.'

Too busy day-dreaming. Missed my chance again. Stupid fool. You know what they say,

11

'faint heart never won…' She's coming over. She's going to speak.

'Are you coming next week?'

'Umm, yes… yes… I think I might.'

'See you then.'

She spoke to me. I want to tell her I'll pick her up. That I'll drive over to her place. Lay soft rugs in the car and when she sits down I'll have the radio playing gently, 'Misty' and 'Can't take my eyes off you', and 'String of Pearls' played with a big band sound. I'll give her a small present, maybe a corsage of white orchids, that would be nice and she'll look at me and we'll know that we are returning to her place. And I'll just take her hand. That smooth sweet hand with the perfectly polished nails and I'll kiss the tips then run one finger down the length of her arm pulling her towards me and those wonderfully yielding lips. And I'll be holding her and she'll be making gentle sounds and…

But now the words stumble in my mouth. I can't say anything. I'm afraid to go any further. She buys her ticket and I follow with

all my speech straight-jacketed in my throat. I'm like a young lad behind the bike-sheds wanting to look, wanting to touch, afraid to go any further.

I thought she turned around then. No. There's Dai running after her and she's smiling at him. She's getting into his car. Well, that's it then.

I change – it's dark now. Too late to do anything outside. I'll check my orders for seeds and note if I need anything else. But the house feels dark and empty, kind of hollow and suddenly I hate my familiar surroundings. It's been years since I felt like this.

A tap at the door. It's Vicky. She's holding a casserole dish.

'You look a bit glum, Dad. No luck tonight?'

'I'm wasting my time. There's only one there worth bothering with, and she's so popular she wouldn't be interested in the likes of me.'

'Don't knock yourself, Dad. Look, I had an idea. I made these cards for you at my night-school computer class – good aren't they?

They've got your name, address and phone number. Just slip her a card and write a little message on the back. Then, if she likes you… well…' She pushes a small plastic envelope into my hand.

'Don't forget to eat that casserole – it's chicken, your favourite. I'll be in tomorrow. See you then, love.'

The door slams and the walls start creeping at me. I switch on Coronation Street – Maggie used to like it, pour a beer and pretend I'm at the Rovers.

A week later, going to the tea-dance. I've got one of Vicky's cards in my pocket and I've written a message. 'Do you fancy a drink or coffee, sometime?' Walking in, she's sitting at her usual table. I'll just hand her the card… steady boy…my hands are shaking like a young lad's…just hand her the bloody note!

'It's Alice, isn't it? I just thought…' I pass her the card. She seems pleased but I don't wait. She might laugh at an old fool like me. Vicky says not to be so daft. I'm not old, just

a slightly-used motor that's been parked up for too long.

I might go and ask her for a dance tonight. Oh damn, it's Dai. He's sat down next to her and she's smiling. Well, there's no point in staying. It hurts me to watch them. I could just get a few potatoes in before the dusk crawls in and the ice sets cold on the ground. I walk past trying not to look and I'm back at the house. I change into gardening clothes and I'm getting into my wellies to concentrate on the winter planting. Vicky's wrong, she's wrong.

Was that a tap at the door? That's not Vicky's knock or the little ones' hammering. I'd better check. I open the door. It's Alice. She's looking pink and plump and marvelous, like a goddess.

'Good gracious, you don't half give a girl a run for her money? she says, all breathy.

'Alice?'

'Well, I've given you enough hints. But at last that card…and then you walk out.' What were you thinking of?'

'But Dai, Dai's your partner.'

'Not at all – he sits down next to me and a girl's got to be polite. Can I come in then?'

And she's in my front room. Alice, here at last taking off her coat, sitting on my couch, smiling at me, just me! And suddenly my room is lit so bright with a luminescence as if all the chandeliers at the Waldorf Astoria are sparking and glittering with shining light.